First American Edition 1991 by Kane/Miller Book Publishers
Brooklyn, New York & La Jolla, California

Originally published in Japan in 1989 under the title *Ojiichan no Machi*
by Kodansha Ltd., Publishers, Tokyo, Japan

Library of Congress Cataloging-in-Publication Data

Nomura, Takaaki, 1949-
   [Ojīchan no machi. English]
   Grandpa's town / by Takaaki Nomure : translated by Amanda Mayer
Stinchecum. — 1st American ed.
      p.   cm.
   Translation of: Ojīchan no machi.
   Summary: A young Japanese boy, worried that his grandfather is
lonely, accompanies him to the public bath.
   ISBN 0-916291-36-7
   [1. Grandfathers—Fiction.   2. Baths—Fiction.   3. Loneliness—
Fiction.   4. Japan—Fiction.]   I. Title.
PZ7.N73Gr   1991
[E]—dc 20
                                     91-13431
                                         CIP
                                         AC

Printed and bound in Italy by New Interlitho S.P.A. Milan
1 2 3 4 5 6 7 8 9 10

Grandpa's Town

By Takaaki Nomura

Translated by Amanda Mayer Stinchecum

A CRANKY NELL BOOK

 Kane/Miller Book Publishers
Brooklyn, New York & La Jolla, California

ぼくの　おじいちゃんは、おばあちゃんが
なくなってから、もう　いちねんも、
ひとりで　この　まちで　くらして　いる。
おかあさんと　ぼくは、ひさしぶりに
おじいちゃんの　いえに　やって　きた。
「おとうさん　ひとりで　たいへんですから、
わたしたちの　いえに　きて　くださいね。」
と、おかあさんが　いうと、
「わしは　ここで　くらすで　いいよ。」
と、おじいちゃんは　すまして　いった。
そして、
「さあ、ふろやに　いくぞ。」
と、ぼくに　あいずを　した。

Grandpa lived alone in his town for a year now,
ever since Grandma died. Mommy and I had just
come to visit him for the first time in a long while.

"It must be terrible for you to be all alone here,
Father," Mommy said to him. "Why don't you come
stay at our house?"

"Living here is okay, really," was all Grandpa
answered.

After awhile he announced, "Well, I'm going to
the public bath. Do you want to come along?"

いえを でると、おじいちゃんは、
「おまえの おかあさんは こわいなあ」
と いった。
「でも、おじいちゃんの こと、みんなで
いつも しんぱいしてるよ。」
と、ぼくは こたえた。
こんどは ぼくが、
「ひとりぼっちで さみしく ないの。」
と きいたら、おじいちゃんは、
「へいきだぞ。」
と、むねを はって あるきだした。

Once we left the house, Grandpa said, "Your mother is really something, isn't she?"

"It's just that everybody's worried about you." And then it was my turn to ask, "Aren't you lonely all by yourself?"

"I don't mind," he said, sticking out his chest proudly and marching off.

しばらく あるいて、また ぼくは、
おじいちゃんに きいた。
「どうして ぼくたちと いっしょに
くらさないの。」
おじいちゃんは、「そうだなあ。」
と いった まま、だまって あるいた。

After we had walked a little way, I asked
him again, "Why don't you come and live
with us?"

Grandpa just said, "Hmm . . ." and
walked on without saying anything else.

さかなやさんの　まえを　とおりかかると、
ながぐつを　どたどた　いわせながら、
「おう、げんさんの　まごかい。」って、
たいのような　めだまで、ぼくを
のぞきこんだ　さかなやの　おじさん。
おじいちゃんは、
「とめさん　とこの　まごと　おなじ
ぐらいかなあ。」
と、にっこり　わらった。

We came to the fish store. Making a plop plop noise with his rubber boots, and with big eyes bulging so that he looked like a fish himself, the fish man said, "So, Gen, this is your grandson."

"I guess, Tome, he's about the same age as your grandson," Grandpa said with a grin.

やおやさんの まえに くると、
「おっ、げんさん、ふろですか。
かわいい まごも いっしょだな、
なまえは なんて いうんだい。
ふろの かえりにゃあ、また よんなよ。
まっかな ほっぺみたいな りんご、
あげるからよっ。」
と、ぺらぺら しゃべった、めがねの
めが やさしい、やおやの おじさん。

When we reached the greengrocer's store, the vegetable man started chattering to us. "On your way to the bath, Gen? Is that your grandson with you? What's his name? Drop by on your way back from the bath so I can give you a bright red apple just like your cheeks."

The greengrocer's eyes looked kind behind his glasses.

おふろやさんの のれんを くぐる。
「あら、げんさん、ずいぶん はやいねえ」
と、おどろいたような ばんだいの おばさん。
「きょうは、おとな ひとりと、
こども ひとり」
と、おじいちゃんは にこにこ いった。
「おや、おまごさん」
と、おばさんは おつりを だしながら、
おじいちゃんの うしろに かくれて いる
ぼくを のぞきこんだ。

We ducked under the curtains outside the bath.

"My, Gen, you're very early today," the lady in the attendant's booth exclaimed, as if she was surprised.

"One adult and one child today," Grandpa said with a smile.

Spotting me hiding behind Grandpa, she said, "Oh, your grandson!" as she handed him his change.

はじめて はいった おふろやさんに、
ぼくは うれしいような こわいような。
ふろばは、もやもや ゆげが いっぱい。
ぼくは、どきどき むねが いっぱい。
おじいちゃんは、たたみやの おじさんと
はなしを して いる。
「げんさんの まごかい。
うちの ごんたより ちょっと
ちっちゃいかなあ。」
と、おじさんが いった。
その うしろに いた おにいちゃんが、
ぼくを にらんだ。

I felt both happy and scared going into the public bath in Grandpa's town for the first time. The bathing room was all foggy with steam. My heart thumped in my chest. Grandpa meanwhile was talking to the tatami-mat maker.

"Is this your grandson, Gen? He's just a little bit younger than our Gonta," the tatami-mat maker said.

Gonta was standing behind his father glaring at me.

おじいちゃんと ぼくは、せなかを
あらいっこする。
おじいちゃんは たたみやの おじさんに、
「まごに あらって もらうのは
いい もんだなあ、きっつあん。」
と、うかれがおに なる。
きょろきょろして いる ぼくに、
いたずらにいちゃんが ちょっかいを だす。
たたみやの おじさんは、
にいちゃんを つかまえて、
「こっちは いつも これだから、
てえへんだあ。」
と、あたまを こづいた。

Grandpa and I scrubbed each other's backs. "Having your grandson wash your back is a great thing, Kitsu," he said to the tatami-mat maker, beaming.

Gonta started to tease me. The tatami-mat maker made him stop.

"He's always like this—a pest," he said, giving him a little poke.

おじいちゃんと　ぼく、そして、たたみやの
おじさん、いたずらにいちゃん、
それに、たてぐやの　おじさんも、
ガラスやの　おじさんも。
みんなで　ゆぶねに　のんびり
つかって　いる。
そこで、おじいちゃんが
「まごの　ゆうたと　ゆうだ。」
と、おどけて　すまして　いったもんだから、
わっはっはって、みんなの　わらいごえが、
てんじょう　たかく、ゆげと　いっしょに
ひろがった。

Grandpa and I, the tatami-mat maker, his pesky son, the cabinetmaker and the man from the plate-glass store—we all soaked in the bath together.

"This is my grandson. He's called Yuuta," Grandpa said, making a silly joke about my name.

"Ha ha ha ha ho ho ho," our laughing voices echoed from the high ceiling and mixed with the steam.

ぼくは おじいちゃんに、
「もう でようよ。」と いった。
はじめてで ちょっと のぼせて しまった。
たたみやの おじさんと、
いたずらにいちゃんに、
「おさきに。」と いったら、
おにいちゃんが にこっと わらって くれた。

おじいちゃんと ぼくが あがって きて
きかえて いるのを、
たてぐやと ガラスやの おじさんが
いっぷくしながら みて いた。

"Let's get out now," I said to Grandpa. I was a little dizzy, because it was my first time in such hot water. "Excuse me, I have to get out now," I said to the tatami-mat maker and his son.

Gonta gave me a friendly smile.

The cabinetmaker and the plate-glass man were taking a break. They watched Grandpa and me get out of the bath and put on our clothes.

ようふくを きてから、ぼくが
おじいちゃんの かたを たたいて いると、
さっきの おじさんたちが、
「げんさん、この まち でるんかい。」
と、こえを かけて きた。
おじいちゃんは しばらく たって、
「いやあ、ずっと この まちに いるよ。」
と いった。
ぼくは いつの まにか、
ちからいっぱい かたを たたいて いた。

We got dressed, and as I pounded Grandpa's shoulders for him, the two men asked, "Are you going to move away, Gen?"

After a long pause, Grandpa answered, "No, I'm in this town for good."

Before I knew what I was doing, I was beating Grandpa's shoulders with all my might. That's how disappointed I felt.

かえる ときに、ばんだいの おばさんが、
「ゆうたくん、また おじいちゃんの
ところに きたら、いっしょに きてね。」
と、こゆびを だした。
ぼくは おじいちゃんの かおを みながら、
ゆびきり げんまん、やくそくを した。

When it was time to leave, the lady in the attendant's booth said, "Next time you come to Grandpa's place, Yuuta, stop by with him again, won't you?"

She stuck out her little finger, to make me promise. Looking at Grandpa's face as I did it, I hooked fingers with her and promised with all my heart.

おふろやさんを　でると、ゆうひが
まっかで　まぶしかった。
おじいちゃんと　ぼくの　ほっぺも、
まっかで　ほっかほか。
そして、おじいちゃんは　タオルを　だして、
「ゆうた、ゆざめしちゃあ　だめだぞ。」
と、かおの　あせを　ふいて　くれた。

When we came out of the bath, the evening sun was a dazzling red. Grandpa and I both had glowing bright red cheeks. "You mustn't catch a chill, Yuuta," he said, as he took out a towel and wiped the sweat off my face.

おじいちゃんと　ぼくは、とおまわりして
かえる　ことに　した。
ぼくは、おじいちゃんの　せなかを
おしながら、ゆっくり　ゆっくり　あるいた。
「おじいちゃん、ひとりぼっちじゃ
ないんだね。」って　いったら、
おじいちゃんは　ふりかえって、
「そうだなあ。」
と、たのしそうに　いった。

Grandpa and I decided to take the long way home. Trudging along slowly, slowly, I pushed Grandpa from behind.

"You aren't alone after all, are you, Grandpa?" I said.

Grandpa looked back over his shoulder at me.

"Hmm hmm . . ." he agreed happily.